SEVEN STORIES

BY ED BRIANT

A Neal Porter Book • ROARING BROOK PRESS • New Milford, Connecticut

Copyright © 2005 by Ed Briant
A Neal Porter Book
Published by Roaring Brook Press
Roaring Brook Press is a division of Holtzbrinck Publishing
Holdings Limited Partnership
143 West Street, New Milford, Connecticut 06776
All rights reserved

Distributed in Canada by H. B. Fenn and Company Ltd.

Roaring Brook Press Books are available for special promotions
and premiums.
For details contact: Director of Special Markets,
Holtzbrinck Publishers.

First edition October 2005
Book design by Jennifer Browne
Printed in China
10 9 8 7 6 5 4 3 2 1

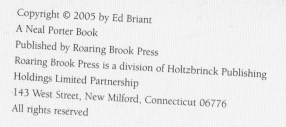

TO ALL INSOMNIACS EVERYWHERE— ESPECIALLY MY MUM

Library of Congress Cataloging-in-Publication Data
Briant, Ed.
Seven stories / written and illustrated by Ed Briant.
p. cm.
Summary: A girl in a seven-story apartment building has trouble sleeping
because of her disruptive neighbors, who all seem to be characters from
fairy tales.
ISBN 1-59643-056-7
[1. Characters in literature—Fiction.   2. Apartment houses—Fiction.]
1. Title.
PZ7.B75883Se 2005
[E]—dc22
2004024351

The clock struck
eight. I turned
over once.

I turned over twice,
and tried to go to sleep.

The clock struck nine, and I heard
a loud clomp in apartment five.

"Fee?"

"Fie!"

"Fo."

Something in the
hall went *Honk*.
A little boy
whispered,
"Hush."

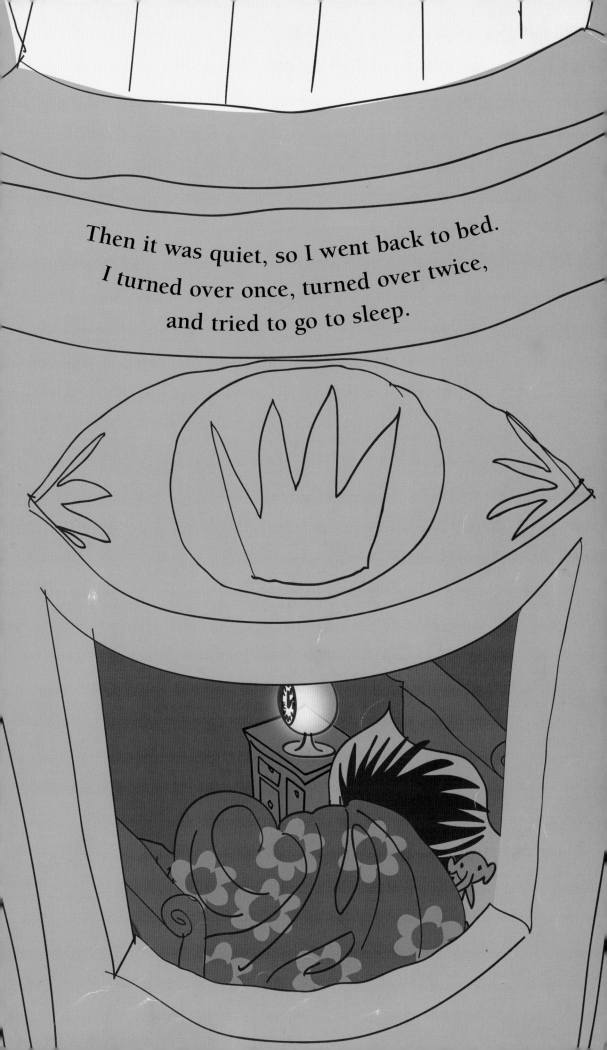

Then it was quiet, so I went back to bed.
I turned over once, turned over twice,
and tried to go to sleep.

At ten o'clock I heard a shriek from apartment three.

"You stay there while
I tend to the oven."

Then I turned over once,
turned over twice.

And tried to go to sleep.

At eleven I woke to find a handsome young man at my window.

"Lovely evening," he said.

"What's wrong with the stairs?" I asked him.

"I need the exercise," he replied.

Just before midnight I heard loud music coming from apartment one. The most beautiful girl I had ever seen was racing out of the building.

I heard
someone calling,
"Please wait."

Then I turned over once,
turned over twice,
and tried to go to sleep.
The clock struck one.

"Someone's been sleeping in *my* bed!" roared a voice from apartment two.

"Someone's been sleeping
in *my* bed, too!"

"Someone's been sleeping in
my bed—and she's still in it!"

I heard footsteps flying
down the stairs.

I was just dropping off at two when a blast of wind sent me flying.

I got up to shut
the window.

"Why don't you come out and play?"

"Not by the hair of our chinny, chin, chins!"

I lifted up my mattress
and found a tiny green pea.
I put the pea carefully
on the windowsill.

Then I turned over
once, turned over
twice. And fell
fast asleep.